Readers will also enjoy:

DIRKLE SMAT
INSIDE MOUNT FLATBOTTOM

and

DIRKLE SMAT
AND THE FLYING STATUE

DIRKLE SMAT
AND THE VIKING SHIELD

And The
Viking Shield

LYNN D. GARTHWAITE

Illustrated by Craig Howarth

CASTLE KEEP PRESS
James A. Rock & Company, Publishers
Rockville, Maryland

Chapter One

Dirkle Smat and Fiddy Bublob stood looking down at the massive remains of a fallen oak tree. Toonie Oobles was the next to arrive and a moment later Bean Lumley rode up with Quid Smat in his sidecar. All five of the Explorers were at the scene.

The quiet bay on Squabble Lake had been named Lone Oak Bay because one single, very old oak tree had grown up on the rocky hillside near the bay. No one in town knew how that one tree had appeared where almost nothing else grew, but it had been there for over a hundred years now and was part of the town's identity.

Dirkle was shocked to see the tree in this condition. The force of the wind from the storm the night before had not only knocked over the huge tree, but had completely pulled up the roots which were now lying on top of the ground. The ball of dirt surrounding the roots was so big, as it lay on its side, that it was taller than Dirkle.

"Yoips!" said Dirkle as he looked at the giant tree.

The Explorers climbed down the side of the hill to inspect the fallen tree more closely.

"I wonder if we can cut off some of these roots," said Quid, poking at them with a stick he found on the ground. "The way they're all twisted and gnarly, they'd make great wall decorations for the club house if we cleaned them up."

"What a cool idea," answered Toonie, and she began to brush some of the dirt away from the roots. They all brushed dirt, exposing the roots to the air for the first time in over a *hundred* years.

Dirkle squinted his eyes, looking more closely at the dirt in front of him. "What's this?" he wondered out loud, as he raked large pieces of dirt from the tangle of roots. He tapped on something metal.

Everyone gasped in surprise when they realized that he was uncovering a square metal box, jammed tightly between the twisted roots.

Fiddy looked closely at the ancient box, wrapped snugly in dirty tree roots. "How could anyone have put *that* there? How did they get it *inside* all those roots?"

"I'm guessing the box was here *first*. Then the tree grew around it," answered Bean. "And since this tree is about 150-years-old, this box has been here at least that long."

"Let's get this thing out of these roots," said Dirkle. "I think we've got a new mystery ahead of us."

Chapter Two

Dirkle was right, they *were* about to start a new mystery. But he had no idea, yet, where it was going to lead. As soon as they got the box back to the clubhouse, Bean started working on the rusted padlock that held the container shut. Using a long pair of pliers and a sewing needle he was able to wiggle around inside the mechanism and pop open the lock.

The Explorers gathered around as he carefully pulled up the metal lid to reveal the contents inside.

"It's just a piece of paper," sighed Fiddy. "I was hoping for some *gold* or jewelry."

"I was hoping for some pictures of aliens," offered Quid.

Dirkle wasn't disappointed at all. With great anticipation, he carefully lifted the paper out of the box and gently unfolded it.

"I think it's a *treasure* map," he said, barely able to breathe with excitement. "And there's a note attached."

Toonie's voice squeaked. "Read it aloud, Dirkle. What does it say?"

Dirkle's eyes flew across the words on the page as he prepared to read it to his friends.

I, Desmond Frank Wobnurt, do hereby bury this map, and all of its secrets on the 28th day of June, 1864. I shall travel to Boston, Massachusetts, in search of an expert in Nordic antiques in order to verify the authenticity of the Viking shield the townspeople have discovered in the hills.

"Wow! A Viking shield! Where is it?" asked Toonie.

"There's more to the note," said Dirkle, and he finished reading.

A small oak sapling shall mark the spot of this map which leads to the place I have buried the shield to keep it safe and secure until my return.

"And then he signed the note at the bottom," said Dirkle, who held it up for everyone to see.

"So Bean was right. The box was buried first and the tree planted over it," Fiddy said. "Now we know how Lone Oak Bay got its tree."

Quid was lost in thought. "I don't get it. Why did he have to hide the shield and find someone to make sure it was real?"

Bean tapped his chin as he searched his memory. "I remember a field trip in first grade to Town Hall where they talked about the mysterious shield. Apparently the town was divided over whether it was real or fake. Some people still didn't believe that the Vikings were here before Christopher Columbus."

"I remember hearing about that too," added Dirkle. "There were some big arguments about the shield and the people who thought it was a fake were planning to destroy it."

"So it sounds like Desmond Wobnurt hid it to protect it," reasoned Toonie.

"And then he went to find someone who could tell them whether or not it was real," said Fiddy, with excitement. "But I wonder what happened? The shield was never found. He must not have come back."

"And there are many people, to this day, who believe the shield never existed," Bean said quietly. "They think the whole story was just a town myth."

"Now we know the answer to the mystery," said Dirkle. "The shield really exists, but it's been hidden all these years."

Toonie's eyes sparkled with delight. "It looks like finding the shield will be our next big adventure."

Chapter Three

The Explorers spent the next half-hour carefully examining the fragile map they found in the metal box.

They had trouble reading Wobnurt's handwriting in places, and the years and moisture had smeared some of the lines on the map.

Then, Bean discovered another problem with the directions.

"We're going to have a major hurdle reaching the place where Wobnurt hid the shield," he reported. "If I'm reading this

correctly, that spot is *under* more than 20 feet of water!"

"What do you mean?" asked Fiddy.

"Do you remember how our history books said that Squabble Lake was formed when they built a dam in 1905? Before that it was just a narrow river running through the valley."

"Yes, I remember," answered Toonie. "There were a couple of farms in the area and the people had to move when they built the dam because the land the farms were on became part of the lake."

"I see what you're saying, Bean," chimed

in Dirkle. "The shield was buried on land that is now part of the lake, so it's completely under water."

Fiddy was upset at this news. "So we don't have any way of getting to the secret spot?"

"I wouldn't say that," grinned Bean. "I think it's time to bring out my latest invention and give it a test run."

Chapter Four

The next day the Explorers met at the lake.

Bean had attached a trailer to the back of his roto-scooter and sitting on the trailer was a bright red mini-submarine. He was busy attaching a metal claw to the front of it when everyone else arrived.

"That is so cool!" exclaimed Quid. "You've built a submarine!"

"That's right," replied Bean. "My original plan was for us to use it to look for interesting creatures in the lake, but with the discovery of the map, we have another use for it right away."

"How does that metal claw in front work?" asked Dirkle.

"It's got several purposes," explained Bean. "It has a scoop for digging and a claw for holding. My plan is that we use the scoop to uncover the shield and the claw to hold it while we come back to the surface. The controls inside are really very simple."

Quid peeked inside the open hatch on top. "Are we all going to fit in there?"

Bean nodded. "I made it specifically to carry the five of us. It'll be a tight squeeze, but there is a porthole at each seat so everyone will be able to see out while we're under water."

"This is amazing," gasped Toonie. "I can't wait to get going."

"I'm just about ready here," said Bean. "We'll stay on the lake surface while we pace off the number of feet indicated on the map. Then, when we reach the point above

the dig zone, we'll start to dive."

Dirkle dug the map out of his pocket and reviewed it with his fellow Explorers. His finger traced the path that Desmond Wobnurt had drawn for them.

He explained, "According to this map, the dig site is exactly 55 feet from the old grain silo that used to sit in the area. Since the silo is no longer here, Bean and I went to the public library yesterday and checked out some old town maps."

Bean added, "We could see, from the old diagrams, exactly where the grain silo stood. By performing some new calculations, we have concluded that this is the correct launch site. We'll need to go 140 feet from the shoreline to reach our dive zone."

"I'm glad you guys are good at math," responded Quid. "We wouldn't want to have to dig up the whole lake!"

Dirkle smiled. "We believe we'll be within a couple of feet of the spot where the shield is buried. Let's just hope it's not buried too deep."

With the submarine prepared for duty, the Explorers pushed the trailer down to the edge of the lake where they worked together to lift the bright red sub into the water. Being careful not to tip it, the five climbed in through the hatch on top and settled themselves into Bean's newest invention.

Chapter Five

Built into the dashboard of the tiny sub, Bean had included a compass and a gauge that would count off the number of feet they traveled. Bean reset the counter to zero and started the tiny motor. The mini-sub began to move forward.

Toonie and Quid sat in the back and peeked through the porthole windows to watch their progress as they crossed the lake. Bean manned the steering wheel, keeping the water craft heading in a northerly direction, and Fiddy pulled grapes out

of his backpack and passed them around
to everyone.

Dirkle kept his eye on the gauges, watching as the number of feet passed—10 and
then 20 and pretty soon 50 feet across the
lake.

"We're almost halfway there," he reported, "approaching 70 feet."

Everyone sat silently as Dirkle continued to count off the number of feet. When they reached 140 feet, Bean shut down the motor and the sub drifted quietly on the top of the lake.

"Prepare for dive," said Bean as he reached up and secured the hatch with its waterproof seal. He flipped a couple of switches on the panel and pretty soon the sub and its five occupants began to gently sink below the surface of the lake. Watching through their portholes, the group could see the sky disappear from view as the lake rose up to cover the sub.

The sub rocked a little from some distant waves as they sank toward the bottom. Eventually the light filtering down from the sun above the surface began to disappear as they dove deeper and deeper in the lake. Bean flipped another switch and exterior lights came on, lighting up the water around them.

They kept sinking down, down, down.

Fish of all kinds swam by to watch the strange tube with five kids inside and the explorers had fun trying to identify the types of fish as they descended.

"Do we know how deep it is here?" asked Toonie. Bean turned to look at the panel in front of him.

"According to my charts it's about 31 feet deep at this part of the lake. We've already descended 22 feet."

"Look at that fish!" cried Quid, and everyone turned to see where he was pointing. The curious fish swam in a circle around the submarine, examining it from all sides and watching silently. The fish was enormous, longer than the submarine, and its mouth had a funny wedge shape.

"I think that's a sturgeon," said Bean. "They're found all over North America and are often the biggest fish in the lake."

"He's as curious about us as we are about him," whispered Toonie, watching every movement of the huge fish.

The kids continued to look for unusual fish as the submarine dropped to the bottom of the lake. They saw a catfish with whiskers and paddlefish that looked a little like sharks. They spotted schools of tiny fish darting together in formation and six or seven carp swimming along the bottom of the lake, looking for food.

With a gentle bump, the sub touched the sandy bottom of the lake and came to a stop.

"Yoips," said Dirkle, amazed at where they were.

Chapter Six

"Are we in the right spot?" asked Quid, straining to see the area around the sub.

Bean consulted his charts and the map. "According to my research, this should be the spot. I'm going to move the sub around the area while everyone looks to see if there is some kind of marker. If you see anything that looks like something might be buried beneath it, holler out."

Bean navigated the sub, making short passes over the bottom of the lake, crisscrossing within a small section.

There was clear evidence that a farm had once occupied this area. They saw the remains of the foundation of an old stone house, the base of a corn silo, and parts of an old tractor that apparently hadn't been moved before the area had been flooded so many years before. But nothing looked like a clue to a buried Viking shield.

The Explorers were just starting to feel a little discouraged when Quid blurted, "Stop Bean! I think this might be it."

Everyone turned to see what Quid had noticed. Barely sticking out of the soft silt of the lake bottom, an unusual formation of iron bars had caught his eye.

"It *does look* like some kind of marker," said Fiddy. "I think those iron bars were placed that way on purpose."

Sure enough the iron bars formed a shape that was like an Indian teepee, wide at the base but pulled together at the top. The bars were held in place by some kind of metal wire which had withheld the years of being underwater. Bean maneuvered the small sub for a closer inspection.

"Quid, I believe you spotted Wobnurt's marker. This looks like the place to dig."

Suddenly an alarm began to clang in the submarine.

Chapter Seven

"What's that?" cried Toonie, her eyes wide with worry.

"Don't worry," responded Bean as he pushed a button which ended the noise. "I installed an alarm to alert me to a low-oxygen situation, but I set it to go off when we were halfway through our supply. I didn't want to take the chance that we might be so involved in our search that we failed to notice when the air supply ran out."

"Do we have enough to continue?" asked Dirkle.

"Yes, assuming this is the correct marker," answered Bean. "We should have enough time to dig up the shield and get back to the surface before the oxygen runs out. Let's see if I can get to those bars and move them aside."

Bean carefully maneuvered the sub and bumped it up against the metal bars arranged on the bottom of the lake. As soon as he came in contact, he began to play with the levers in front of him that operated the claw mounted at the front of the sub. Like the controls of a video game, the levers inside the sub made the claw open and close and turn at different angles.

Luckily, Bean played a lot of video games, so he was skilled at manipulating the claw. Very quickly, he managed to grab onto the iron bars.

"I'll turn the claw command over to you Dirkle. While you maintain the grip on the marker, I'll reverse the sub and see if we can pull it up."

Dirkle grabbed a firm hold on the joystick control while Bean reversed the engine of the tiny sub. By making the sub go backward, they were able to pull at the marker. Little by little, they managed to yank the bars up and out of the sandy bottom of the lake.

When it finally pulled loose, everyone in the sub realized they had been holding their breath in anticipation. Now they all breathed with relief and looked out the window at the front of the sub to see what was below. Where the marker had been was the start of a small hole and they were sure that they had found their treasure.

Dirkle, with his hand on the claw controls, released the marker and watched it settle back to the floor of the lake, several feet away from its former resting place. Now Bean drove the sub gently back to the hole they had uncovered and placed his hands on the levers that controlled the small scoop in front.

Very *carefully,* and with somewhat limited visibility, Bean managed to dig at the hole and make it bigger. Unfortunately every time he moved the scoop it would send clouds of silt through the water, clouding the water and making it very difficult for him to see what he was doing. At some point he turned the controls over to Dirkle so he could continue.

"Keep digging Dirkle," said Bean. "I'm going to work the sub controls to move us even closer to the hole and I need to continue to monitor the gauges."

Toonie, Fiddy and Quid could do nothing but watch and encourage the two as they worked together to enlarge the hole. Little by little they increased the size of the opening in the lake bottom until they finally heard the wonderful "thump" sound of metal hitting hard wood.

Chapter Eight

The inside of the sub was silent as the five explorers froze with excitement.

"Yoips!" said Dirkle. "I think we found it."

No one spoke as Dirkle and Bean maneuvered the sub and the scoop controls to uncover the source of the "thump" sound. Sure enough they found themselves looking at a perfectly round shield made of pine wood and decorated with a variety of Norse symbols. In the center of the shield was a hole which was edged with a metal strip.

"This is so fantastic!" shouted Fiddy. "We *found* it!"

"Now we have to get it out of that hole," reported Bean. "I'll see if I can get the claw to gently grab the edge of the shield. We don't want to damage it in any way."

Working carefully, Bean was able to get the claw wedged down on the edge of the shield and close its fingerlike pieces around it. As he pulled back on the claw spring, the shield lifted from the bottom and floated in the water.

"Bean, I don't want to *worry* you, but look at the oxygen gauge," said Dirkle.

Bean looked down at his panel of gauges and saw that the dial was in the red zone, indicating that they had used up almost all of their oxygen.

"If we can float right back to the surface, we'll be okay," said Bean. "The problem is that I had no way of calculating the weight of this shield when I determined the engine power we would need to drag it up.

This seems to be MUCH heavier than I anticipated."

Sure enough, even though he revved the submarine engine at a high rate, the weight of the Viking shield was keeping them at the bottom of the lake.

Toonie had an idea. "How about if you swish the shield from side to side? Maybe it'll act like a flipper and kind of *swim* upward."

"That's a very *good* idea, Toonie," said Bean. "It's worth a try."

Bean told Dirkle to continue to control the claw that hung onto the shield while he worked with the submarine's engine.

Dirkle did as Toonie suggested, using the controls to make the claw move back and forth in a sweeping motion. Sure enough, the motion of the shield swooshing through the water caused the submarine to rise. Bean coordinated the engines with Dirkle's maneuver and the little submarine rose faster.

The surrounding fish could only look on as the strange tube-shaped contraption, with a round shield attached to a claw in front, swished and swam its way to the surface.

"It worked!" cried Quid. "Smart thinking, Toonie."

As soon as the submarine broke the surface of the lake, Bean opened the hatch and let the fresh air inside. He was then able to drive the sub back, slowly, to the landing. They pulled the Viking shield behind them like an inner tube being towed.

All five Explorers were grateful that they would be standing on dry land again soon.

Once ashore, they were able to examine their find more closely. The shield was made of wood about five inches thick. It was completely round and when they stood it up on end it was about three feet tall. It took all five of them to carry it and strap it onto Bean's trailer.

"We're going to have to go to the library to find out what all these symbols mean," said Fiddy. "I've never seen writing like this."

"And can you imagine how nice this will look displayed at City Hall?" asked Dirkle. "The Mayor won't *believe* what we've found."

"This certainly solves the mystery of whether the shield ever really existed," said

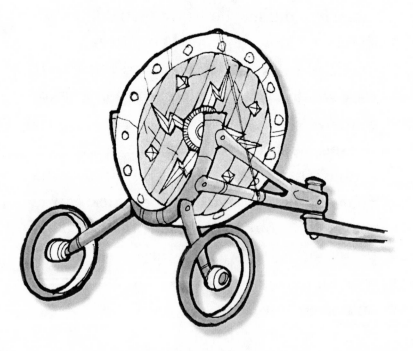

Bean. "It's going to be the talk of the town for another 150 years."

The Explorers all smiled with delight as they mounted their rotoscooters for the ride back into town, towing their treasure behind them.

And on a moonlit night about a week later, a passerby might have noticed five young Explorers burying a metal box on the side of the hill at Lone Oak Bay. The box was now filled with notes and games and knick-knacks that were small treasures to the kids.

As they planted a sturdy oak sapling on top of the box, Dirkle Smat and the Explorers imagined that maybe, in 100 years, some new kids might find their hidden secrets and learn about the adventures of the Explorers Club.

About the Author

Lynn Garthwaite lives in Bloomington, Minnesota with her husband and two sons.

Make Your Own Explorer's Club

Members:

_____

_____

_____

_____

_____

Members:

_____

_____

_____

_____

_____

_____

Equipment:

_____

_____

_____

_____

_____

_____

_____

Adventures:

_____

_____

_____

_____

_____

_____

LaVergne, TN USA
03 November 2009
162866LV00003B/39/P